CW00542894

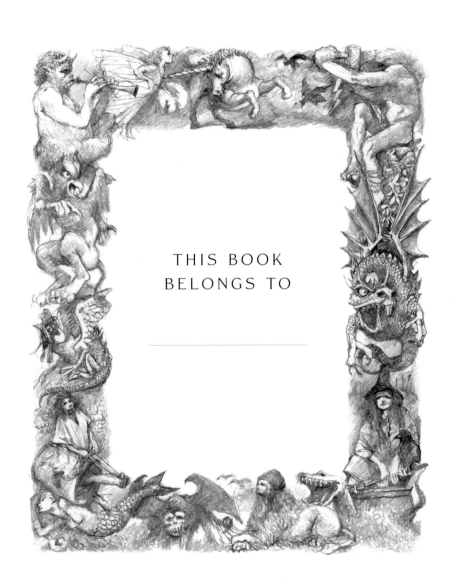

THIS BOOK
BELONGS TO

....

For Marnie and for Sasha.
Thank you for making our world that little bit more magical – **M.E.**

Published in 2023 by Welbeck Editions
An Imprint of Welbeck Children's Limited,
part of the Welbeck Publishing Group
Offices in: London - 20 Mortimer Street, London W1T 3JW
& Sydney - Level 17, 207 Kent St, Sydney NSW 2000 Australia
www.welbeckpublishing.com

Design and layout © Welbeck Children's Limited 2023
Text © 2023 Maz Evans
Illustration © 2023 Robert Ingpen

Maz Evans and Robert Ingpen have asserted their moral rights
to be identified as the author and illustrator of this Work in
accordance with the Copyright Designs and Patents Act 1988.

All rights reserved. No part of this publication may be
reproduced, stored in a retrieval system, or transmitted in any
form or by any means, electronically, mechanical, photocopying,
recording or otherwise, without the prior permission of the
copyright owners and the publishers.

A CIP catalogue record for this book is available from the
British Library.

ISBN 978 1 80338 116 9

Printed in Heshan, China

10 9 8 7 6 5 4 3 2 1

Disclaimer: Any names, characters,
trademarks, service marks and trade
names detailed in this book are the
property of their respective owners
and are used solely for identification
and reference purposes. This book is
a publication of Welbeck Editions,
part of Welbeck Publishing Group
and has not been licensed, approved,
sponsored or endorsed by any
person or entity.

FSC
www.fsc.org
MIX
Paper | Supporting
responsible forestry
FSC® C020056

THE HIDDEN WORLD OF
MAGICAL CREATURES

Written by MAZ EVANS

Illustrated by ROBERT INGPEN

WELBECK
EDITIONS

Long ago the hidden world felt very much closer than it does today. In past days, when church bells were the loudest sound in the countryside, a wanderer through the meadows in the stillness of a midsummer twilight was conscious of a magic which simply does not exist in computer games. The spirits of the earth and trees whispered to us enchanting messages which today are inaudible to our minds, cluttered with the noise and debris of our modern technological world. There could be no doubt that dragons lived in caves, and that fairies and goblins hid in your garden, and unicorns were never far away. Living in the depths of the village pond, the witch Jenny Greenteeth was as easily imagined as the thunder of hoofbeats from a herd of centaurs over the hill. Everyone knew and believed it.

And it was so in every other part of the world. Forests, jungles, mountains, deserts, and the lakes and oceans all have fabulous creatures which live in a dimension different from that of humans and reality. Sometimes these creatures break through the barriers of consciousness and reveal themselves to us.

This book selects and describes a number of the creatures that inhabit that hidden world so that we might perhaps see and hear them once again, and learn how to recognise and respect them.

GRIFFIN

With the head of an eagle and the body of a lion, a griffin is not a creature you want to upset. And nothing upsets a griffin more than human greed.

Griffins once flourished in the deserts of Turkey, Armenia, Syria and Iraq, where lavish jewels sparkled across the sands – and griffins made sure that the greedy humans who sought them soon paid for their avarice. Larger than a lion and fiercer than a hundred eagles, you'd think a griffin would be hard to avoid. But greed is often stronger than fear and many have found a way – over time, the griffins have lost their prey.

Retired from drawing the chariots of gods and with the insatiable appetite of humans stripping the deserts of their riches, these days griffins are scarcely seen. But humans would be wise to ensure that love of their wealth never exceeds love of their world. After all, griffins not being seen is hardly the same as griffins not being here.

PHOENIX

Perfection cannot apparently be improved upon – although that doesn't stop the majestic Phoenix from making its infrequent attempts.

A beautiful creature that has inspired human awe and adoration for millennia, the Phoenix is distinguished not only by his stunning golden plumage, but a singing voice of such sweetness that any audience immediately commits their life to hope and joy. With only one sole specimen alive at any given time, the Phoenix is affable to humans, if not overly concerned with their trivialities. When you have five hundred years to live, most controversies quickly fade into irrelevance.

Indeed, this extended lifespan gives the Phoenix plenty of time to reflect upon any potential enhancements – and his cyclical regeneration grants the opportunity to enact them. For once he feels that his life has come to a useful end, the Phoenix bursts into an incandescent rainbow of flames. He is then born again from its own ashes in the firm hope that he – and the world around him – can do even better this time.

CENTAUR

While many creatures face dangers from without, there are two threats from within their own community of which all centaurs should be aware. The first is wine. The second is each other.

It is a story to be found across creation – a centaur is noble, good and wise... until it drinks too much. Once a familiar sight galloping the mountain slopes of Grecian Thessaly, the centaur cut a magnificent figure, its muscular masculine torso powered by the equine legs of a thoroughbred stallion.

The modern centaur is certainly no less physically imposing. But a weakness for wine has led to a certain lawlessness, earning the centaurs a dubious reputation that they richly deserve and thoroughly enjoy. Centaurs truly know how to have a good time – they just don't know how to stop. This leads to frequent and widespread brawling, which can be heard for miles and last for days.

The good news is that centaurs rarely hold grudges and peace is soon restored. The bad news is that this good will is usually celebrated with several more flasks of wine.

SPHINX

It is generally accepted in this life that sometimes you win, and sometimes you lose. And in fairness to the sphinx, it has fully accepted half of this maxim.

Wrongly believed to be exclusively female, a sphinx can in fact assume any gender it wishes. All sphinx have the body of a lion – the Grecian sphinx may have the wings of an eagle, the Egyptian sphinx may not, but it can change its mind on this as it does on most other matters.

The sphinx enjoys little more than the cut and thrust of intellectual conversation, loving to challenge its visitors with a riddle. Lamentably, it also enjoys the cut and thrust of killing those who can't solve them, so anyone engaging with a sphinx should keep their wits – and possibly some weaponry – about them.

However, were you brave or foolish enough to criticise these capricious beasts, it's fair to say that they are not the best losers. Should you defeat them at their battle of wits, they really take it to heart – their own, in fact, which will most likely implode from their humiliated fury.

MERFOLK

Humans often speak of their desire to have the best of both worlds –
merfolk have perhaps achieved this elusive ideal.

Originally from the shores of Brittany, the merfolks' natural curiosity
took them across the English Channel, where they were named mermaids
and mermen. They are most comfortable beneath the waves, where their
iridescent tails can power them effortlessly down rivers or across oceans.

But their amphibian nature also allows them brief sojourns on dry land,
with rumours that some are able to grow legs for the purpose. However,
they must be cautious not to stray too far from water lest they become
stranded on land, forced to disguise themselves as other sea
creatures to keep their secret world hidden from the human gaze.

Merfolk are gifted musicians, but you might wish to enjoy their
talents from afar. Human mistreatment of the oceans has made
them hostile to our species and, despite the fairy tales, merfolk are
far more likely to be the cause of a shipwreck than a saviour of it.

DRAGON

The dragon can surely claim the prize for having the greatest variety within a single species. And even if it doesn't – who would want to argue with it?

Born from reptiles and fear, the dragon is as likely to be found soaring through the heavens as slinking through a forest, gliding through the deepest ocean and scaling the tallest mountain. They have been known to migrate, although remain largely confined to the continents of Asia, Africa and Europe, especially in places where they are least likely to encounter humans.

But there is one gift all dragons share. Once an infant dragon has seen its third winter, it quickly develops the power to breathe fire. This ability can take several years to master and accidents are plentiful, so it is wise to give dragons a wide berth during their teenage years.

Humans have been known to discover abandoned dragon eggs (there are no reported survivors from those who attempted to take them from their mothers) and rear the young as pets. A baby dragon can indeed make a delightful addition to a family. At least, until its third winter.

HARPY

Hell hath no fury like a woman scorned – and if you hear the scream of a harpy, you may elect to take your chances with the hellfires.

With a long history of dispensing justice to those who thought they had evaded it, the harpy is a righter of wrongs in an unfair world. An avine avenger, the harpy swoops on her prey like fear itself, clutching the wrongdoer in her eagle talons and dispatching them to eternal damnation.

Theirs is not a subtle or stealthy approach. The harpy's inhuman screeches and foul stench give the perpetrator fair warning of the fate that awaits them, even if nothing can prepare them for what they find there. If your own conscience isn't sufficient reminder of your crime, staring into the fearful face of a harpy is an excellent reminder.

Once the instruments of the Greek gods, the harpies intended to retire the moment the human race was free from unpunished souls. They have long since abandoned that hope, patrolling the Earth to ensure that, one way or another, justice is always served.

UNICORN

As is true of any of us, each unicorn is unique to its time and place. Ancient Greek unicorns were white with a purple head. A Chinese unicorn, or *Ki-lin*, has the body of a deer, the hooves of a horse and a voice like a deep bell. In Europe, they are pure white horses with a goatlike beard, a lion's tail and a long, spiralled horn. But all unicorns share a particular affinity with young women. While hunters have eternally tried to ensnare these fleet-footed beauties in their traps, the only way a unicorn will submit to a human, is to lay its head in a young girl's lap.

Once roaming freely around Europe, Asia and Africa, unicorns soon faced the greatest threat imaginable from humans: they proved useful to them. Poison drunk from a unicorn horn loses all its power – but a unicorn without a horn is devoid of power too. Unicorns are now incredibly rare and sightings are scarce. But – just like the young women it so favours – if you encounter one, you should never underestimate its strength.

MANTICORE

Searching for the merits of encountering a manticore, it can at least be said that it is not a wasteful creature. After all, so efficient is it at devouring its prey with its three rows of razor-sharp teeth, it leaves not even a grain of bone behind.

Stalking the forests of India, the manticore boasts an impressive physical armoury to kill its quarry. In the unlikely event of a manticore's teeth proving unequal to the task, the claws of its leonine body are very effective at tearing flesh apart. Failing that, the poison darts in the manticore's tail, dripping with the venom from the upas tree, are an outstandingly efficient last resort.

The elephant and lion alone have evaded the manticore's ferocious clutches – it is otherwise indiscriminate in its diet. It is said that the manticore has a particular taste for human flesh, delighting in gorging on several people in a single sitting. However, such reports are impossible to substantiate – witnesses to these alleged massacres are notoriously hard to come by.

YETI

Few creatures are as elusive, nor as misunderstood as the yeti, which can largely be found (or not) roaming the frozen landscapes of the Himalayas, although they have also been traced to the frozen forests of North America.

Identified through history as the "abominable snowman", "bigfoot" or "migoi", the yeti's form is as unclear as its function. Purported to be apelike in shape and covered in fur that can be white, black or all shades between, this imposing biped can grow to heights of seven feet.

It has been depicted as everything from a malevolent maneater to a peaceful herbivore. What is clear is that it wishes to be left alone. And when a seven-foot creature of unclear nature asks you to respect its privacy, it's probably as well to agree.

BASILISK

Accounts as to how a basilisk comes into being vary widely. Some say it is born of a stolen cockerel's egg, hatched by a serpent. Others believe it is the cockerel that is the thief, deviously incubating the egg of a snake. Both endeavours are as mysterious as they are misguided, for the result is as unfortunate in either scenario.

What the basilisk lacks in size – it is said to be no more than 12 fingers long – it amply compensates for in fury. Its gaze alone can take life – animals have the opportunity not to make eye contact with its deadly stare, plants are not so fortunate. But neither can escape the basilisk's teeth, which are so full of venom that should they touch a spear, they would not only kill the bearer of that weapon, but the horse upon which they are riding.

But nature loves an antidote and the basilisk does have a weakness – the scent of the humble weasel, which is highly toxic to this otherwise indiscriminate killer. One of these small mammals applied to a basilisk's lair is the quickest and most convenient cure for this scourge for all concerned. Except, perhaps, the unfortunate weasel.

KELPIE

There are many reasons to be cautious around large stretches of open water – and should you be fortunate enough to find yourself near the majestic beauty of a Scottish loch, the kelpie is one to add to your list.

An enchanted shape-shifter, the kelpie may appear either as a human with water weeds in their hair or in equine form, the latter making themselves known as a mighty black stallion. In either scenario, it's as well not to dwell too long, lest you find yourself dragged into the waters of the loch, only to emerge in pieces the following day.

Not all kelpies have malevolent intent – some have been known to befriend and even to marry their human visitors. But as with all interactions, you'd be wise to get to know them thoroughly before spending too much time with a kelpie. After all no one wants to be left, either metaphorically or literally, in bits.

THE WILD HUNT

It's no easy task being an immortal god, so on the rare occasions time allows, Odin enjoys little more than a run out with his hounds.

These outings are shrouded in secrecy and very little hard evidence exists of their nature. Some say the Norse god rides with black hounds sporting fire-red eyes, others that the dogs are white with red ears and eyes like silver mirrors. The limited descriptions suggest they are fleet-footed, moving with the speed of the wind and always accompanied by the foreboding presence of Odin's beloved ravens, Hugin and Munin.

Unfortunately, merely seeing the hunt is a harbinger of death and destruction, most commonly, your own. The good news is that on a fortunate day, you may just be spirited away to an enchanted realm for eternity. In any case it's probably as well in this, to simply mind one's own business.

WEREWOLF

The classical image of a werewolf howling at the full moon is as famous as it is false. In truth, the transformation into this fearsome beast can happen manifold ways at any time, giving werewolves a pleasing flexibility about how and when they terrorise their habitats.

You can simply be born a werewolf, or turned into one by magic in the form of a bite or scratch from another werewolf, or by wearing an enchanted wolf's skin. For some this is a gift they celebrate, for others a curse they cannot abide.

Few effective remedies have been found – wolfsbane has been known to act medicinally, but its results are inconsistent and unreliable. Most other attempted cures, usually surgical in nature, while effective at killing the inner werewolf, tend to carry the less desirable side effect of also destroying the outer human.

But the full moon remains a powerful totem for the werewolf and care should be taken on these enchanted evenings. Although capable of devouring flesh on any night of the month, there remains a certain regard for observing this lunar tradition, not least as the light is so much better for seeing what – or whom – they are eating.

CUNMERRIE

A midnight feast is generally considered one of life's greater pleasures. Although if you are unfortunate enough to be in the vicinity of the vicious Cunmerrie when it fancies a nocturnal nibble, you may quickly change your mind.

This scourge of the Northern Australian skyline could easily be mistaken for a bird of prey – several in fact, boasting as it does the head of an owl and the body and wings of an eagle. But whereas smaller quarry may need to exercise caution during the nighttime hours, it is much larger prey at risk from the massive Cunmerrie, which seeks out livestock being herded across the plains and carries off whole cattle or sheep to sate its immense appetite.

VALKYRIE

As with so many moments in this life, the arrival of a valkyrie in your world is both good news and bad. The glad tidings are that you have just been selected to spend a glorious eternity in the Norse afterlife of Valhalla. On the flip side, you have probably just died a violent and gory death on the battlefield. So as with so many moments in this life, you just have to take the rough with the smooth.

The valkyrie cuts an impressive figure – a warrior maiden astride a flying horse, a trail of light blazing through the horrors of war in her shining armour. She is scrupulously fair – unless of course she doesn't like you – constantly monitoring the fighting for particular deeds of valour, those deserving of a seat in the Hall of the Slain.

The valkyrie is a gracious hostess, personally serving her chosen warriors at their bountiful and seemingly endless feast. But the warriors must stay on alert – they will ultimately be called upon to fight alongside Odin and Thor at Ragnarök, the battle that will signal the end of the days. Thus in death, as in life, there is truly no such thing as a free lunch.

BANSHEE

Nobody wants to hear bad news and conventional wisdom tells us that being a messenger can be a risky business. So it is the unfortunate lot of the banshee to be the eternal bearer of bad tidings – although not as unfortunate as the audience for her distinctive and deadly cry.

The banshee is an elusive creature. Sporadic sightings report wild hair that is darker than night, with piercing eyes turned red from weeping. The banshee may be found all around the British Isles, from the highlands of Scotland to the Welsh valleys, with many Irish banshees echoing around the Emerald Isle. Each takes care of their own in their unique style, announcing their presence with an anguished scream, variously believed to resemble the howl of a wolf, the call of the wild geese and the wail of an abandoned child.

But however the message is delivered, the content is always the same: if you hear the cry of the banshee, a family member is doomed to death. So be very afraid should you hear her tormented screams. But be even more so if a relative hears them first.

GIANT

In a world plagued by an obsession with appearance, spare a thought for the noble giant, whose size has been the subject of scrutiny and misunderstanding for millennia. Ever since their earliest ancestors were rejected by their own father Uranus, giants have been forced to live on society's outskirts, their towering presence threatening those smaller in stature and outlook.

Like any community, giants have their rogue elements and it is the most unpleasant of their kind that have attracted the most attention. But in general, giants are a gentle and kind people, using their natural strength to help their more diminutive human neighbours with projects beyond their abilities.

Modest in nature, giants tend not to draw attention to their feats. But next time you see an impossibly tall structure, perhaps you might take a moment to consider how it really got there.

CHARON

Bad-tempered transport employees are not an uncommon feature of human life, but should you encounter Charon, you too might not be having your best day.

This immortal ancient Greek ferryman has been charged down the ages with shipping the souls of the dead across the River Styx to the Underworld. The fare is a single obol, placed beneath the tongue of the deceased to ensure Charon is paid for his work.

But in death, as in life, buying a ticket doesn't always guarantee you a seat. Charon alone decides who earns passage on his boat and has no qualms leaving wretched souls on the banks until he deigns to transport them, or not. If there is a system, or a timetable, no one has ever been made aware of it. So maybe there is some comfort to be found in the fact that some things never change.

ROC

The Indian Ocean has many beautiful sights to commend it, but one you may wish to avoid is the fearsome roc.

This mighty bird of prey, as encountered by Sinbad on his second voyage, is as immense as it is strong. Its feathers alone are twelve paces long and it thinks nothing of carrying off an elephant, or even a ship, in its enormous talons.

The roc can be a terrifying prospect for the seagoing community – although canny sailors have used its unique talents to their advantage. Shipwrecked voyagers have been known to harness the strength of the roc to escape their plights, dressing themselves in cattle skin so that the bird will swoop down and fly them away. This is an ingenious strategy to save them from certain death – at least until the roc discovers that its quarry isn't quite what it seems, at which point the plan can fall quickly apart.

WITCH

Perhaps the only thing more powerful than a witch's magic is the damage done to her reputation by fear. Largely, although not exclusively, female, witches have been blessed with an ability to heal through nature. And thus the witch – whose very name is derived from the Anglo-Saxon word for knowledge – has long been a figure to whom those who conventional wisdom has failed might turn.

But convention doesn't like to be challenged: what it doesn't understand, it seeks to eliminate. Few weapons are more powerful than the wrong words in the right ears and witches have been at their mercy for centuries.

Despite history's best efforts, however, witches continue to proffer healing and wisdom behind the safety of disguises. They are not immune from misusing their gifts, however. On the rare occasions when they deem it necessary, can anyone really blame them for dispensing the occasional piece of frog-related justice?

IFRIT

K nown by many names and renowned for many deeds, the ifrit is a cryptic creature, whose purpose and intent remain shrouded in mystery.

Often denizens of the underworld, the ifrit are considered by many to be malicious and demonic presences, threatening innocents with their fiery figures, clawed hands and sharp horns. To others, they are the spirits of the dead, their character mirroring their death – a natural death creates a peaceful ifrit, whereas a violent one unleashes a vengeful spirit.

But to some, the ifrit is dispensing a higher justice, its fearful methods a fitting end for the wrongdoers it has been sent to punish. As is so often the case with felons, just because they don't care for the means, that doesn't necessarily mean that the ends aren't justified.

KRAKEN

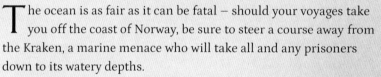

The ocean is as fair as it can be fatal – should your voyages take you off the coast of Norway, be sure to steer a course away from the Kraken, a marine menace who will take all and any prisoners down to its watery depths.

No one is entirely sure why the Kraken is the scourge of sailors, but then no one has remained in its presence long enough to ask. This giant octopus scours the ocean in search of ships to state its vast appetite, offering them a one-way voyage to Davy Jones' locker.

There are few warning signs – the waves appearing to boil on the horizon can be a harbinger of the Kraken's ascent – but in truth, by the time they are observed, it is usually too late. For once it has broken the ocean's surface, the conclusion is foregone. The Kraken wraps its titanic tentacles around the ship and drags it, and all aboard, back to its underwater realm, to the general approval of the marine life so mistreated by the landlubbers.

WENDIGO

While we generally worry about the malevolence we find outside ourselves, we'd all do well to worry more about what evil lurks within. The forest-dwelling wendigo knows how to use this to its cunning advantage, lurking in the shadows behind unwary travellers, before inhabiting their bodies and committing unspeakable wrongs in their name.

There are few clues to the wendigo's presence, but should you find yourself in the plains of North America, you must be alert to their existence. Composed largely of an icy heart, the wendigo emits a strong chill before occupying its victims – not to mention a foul stench.

But the sad truth is that, should you even notice these precursors, you are probably already too late. The best you can hope for is that the defence "a wendigo made me do it" meets sympathetic and enlightened ears.

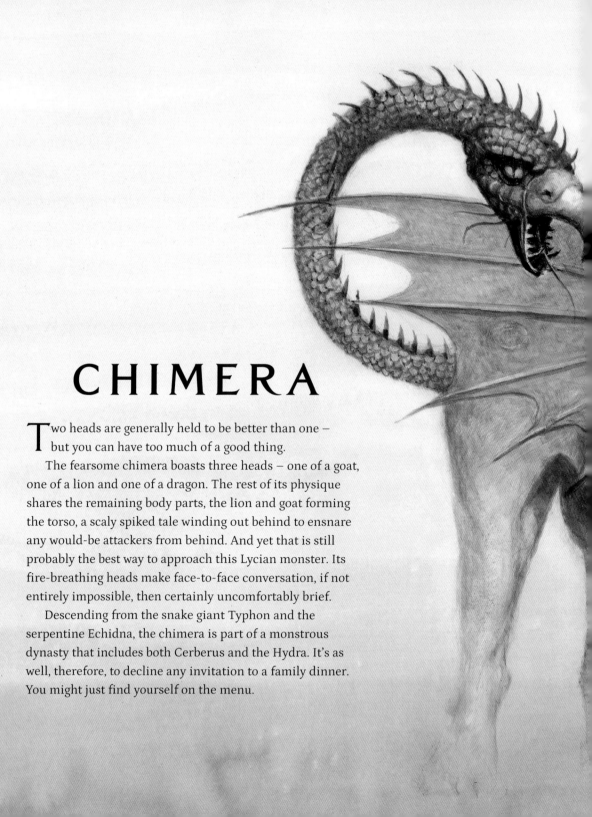

CHIMERA

Two heads are generally held to be better than one – but you can have too much of a good thing.

The fearsome chimera boasts three heads – one of a goat, one of a lion and one of a dragon. The rest of its physique shares the remaining body parts, the lion and goat forming the torso, a scaly spiked tale winding out behind to ensnare any would-be attackers from behind. And yet that is still probably the best way to approach this Lycian monster. Its fire-breathing heads make face-to-face conversation, if not entirely impossible, then certainly uncomfortably brief.

Descending from the snake giant Typhon and the serpentine Echidna, the chimera is part of a monstrous dynasty that includes both Cerberus and the Hydra. It's as well, therefore, to decline any invitation to a family dinner. You might just find yourself on the menu.

BABA YAGA

Elderly women living alone in the forest are rarely treated kindly by the world at large. So when all you aspire to do is live in peace, creative strategies might be required to keep the world at bay. Developing a reputation for eating children would be an effective example and thus Baba Yaga is these days largely left to her own devices.

Whether by choice or necessity, Baba Yaga is often on the move, either astride her flying pestle and mortar or inside her house, by virtue of it being on chicken legs. She can be a wise and helpful aid to the lost traveller, her affinity with nature providing her with magic at her fingertips and sound advice in her heart.

In fairness, she is not always so beneficent and reports of her variously dispensing with, or even eating, unwelcome visitors may not be without basis. But we all have our off days. And who amongst us really likes unwelcome, or unpleasant visitors to our door?

FAUN

The forest is a magical place – so long as you're in the right company. Should you lose your way on a sylvian stroll, you might be fortunate enough to cross paths with a faun.

These playful woodland citizens have been known to help humans – after all, we have a lot in common, namely our head, arms and torso. But goat-like legs and horns make fauns feel more comfortable in nature and that is where they are to be found, especially if you are lost.

Listen out for their music on the woodland breeze – they are skilled in the flute and pipes – but be a little cautious too. These impish folk enjoy nothing more than a magical prank, so check you don't leave your encounter with the head of a donkey. And keep your personal possessions close – courtesy of their inner goat, fauns will happily chew on anything you have to offer, even if you are still wearing it.

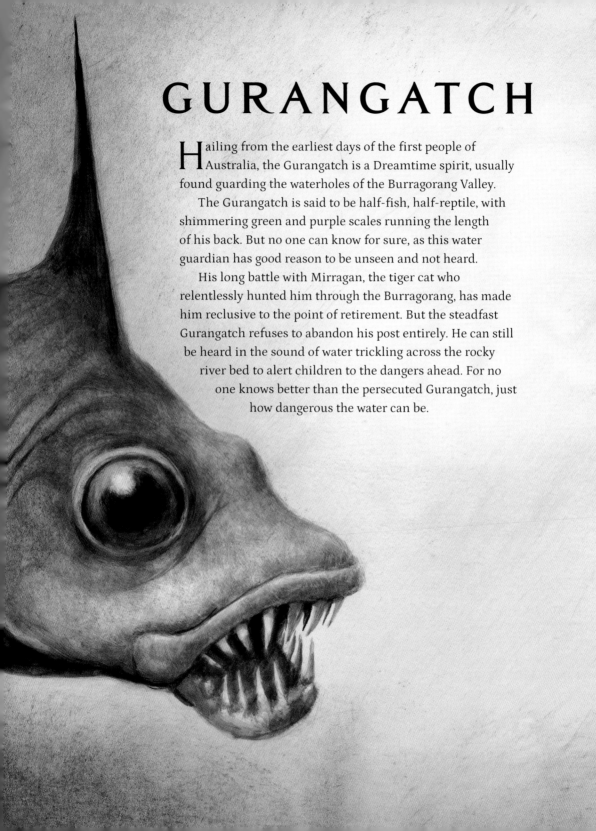

GURANGATCH

Hailing from the earliest days of the first people of
Australia, the Gurangatch is a Dreamtime spirit, usually
found guarding the waterholes of the Burragorang Valley.

The Gurangatch is said to be half-fish, half-reptile, with
shimmering green and purple scales running the length
of his back. But no one can know for sure, as this water
guardian has good reason to be unseen and not heard.

His long battle with Mirragan, the tiger cat who
relentlessly hunted him through the Burragorang, has made
him reclusive to the point of retirement. But the steadfast
Gurangatch refuses to abandon his post entirely. He can still
be heard in the sound of water trickling across the rocky
river bed to alert children to the dangers ahead. For no
one knows better than the persecuted Gurangatch, just
how dangerous the water can be.

GLOSSARY

AFFABLE to be friendly and good-natured

AFFINITY a natural liking for something

AVARICE an extreme greed for wealth

BRITTANY an area in France, bordering the English Channel

BURRAGORANG VALLEY a place in New South Wales, Australia

CAPRICIOUS given to sudden changes in mood or behaviour

CERBERUS the three-headed watchdog of the Greek underworld

CONTROVERSY a disagreement

CRYPTIC to have a meaning that is mysterious

CYCLICAL occurring in cycles

DAMNATION to be condemned to eternal punishment

DAVY JONES' LOCKER a term used by sailors for the darkest depths of the ocean

DEMONIC something that behaves in an evil manner

DREAMTIME the stories of the beginning of the world from ancient Australian peoples

DIMINUTIVE to be extremely or unusually small

DENIZEN a person that lives in a particular place

ECHIDNA an ancient Greek monster that was half woman and half snake

EQUINE relating to horses or members of the horse family

FELON a person who has committed a crime

FOREBODING a feeling that something bad might happen

HARBINGER a person or thing that announces the approach of another

HYDRA a many-headed monster from Greek mythology

INCANDESCENT to emit light as a result of getting hot

INDISCRIMINATE a deed done without careful thought or judgment

INSATIABLE an appetite that is impossible to satisfy

IRIDESCENT showing colours that seem to change if seen from different angles

IRRELEVANCE a lack of importance to a situation

LANDLUBBER a person unfamiliar with the sea or sailing

LAVISH something that is sumptuously rich

LEONINE resembling a lion

LITERAL taking words to mean their usual or most basic sense

LOCH a lake in Scotland

LYCIAN relating to the ancient region of Lycia, now in modern Turkey

MALEVOLENT having a wish to do evil to other people

MALICIOUS to be spiteful or intending to do harm

MAXIM a short statement that expresses a truth or a rule

METAPHORICAL using words to describe or symbolise another thing

MILLENNIA a period of a thousand years

PERPETRATOR a person who carries out a harmful act

PHYSIQUE the form, size and development of a person's body

RAGNARÖK in Norse mythology, the name for the end of the world

REGENERATION something made new again

RIVER STYX a river in the Greek underworld that the souls of the dead must cross

SCOURGE to devastate

SOJOURN a temporary stay

SPORADIC something that is scattered or an event that doesn't occur regularly

SUBSTANTIATE to provide evidence of something

SYLVIAN to be within, or living in, woodland or forest

THESSALY a place in the ancient Greek world

TRIVIALITY to lack seriousness or importance

TYPHON a fearsome many-headed god in ancient Greek mythology, also known as the father of all monsters

UPAS TREE a tree which grows in parts of Africa and Asia with poisonous sap, once used on the tip of darts and arrows

URANUS (GREEK GOD) the ancient Greek god of the sky

VALHALLA in Norse mythology, this was the 'hall of the slain' where warriors were taken after death to await Ragnarök

WOLFSBANE a toxic plant that grows in parts of Europe